Little Princess

THIS BOOK BELONGS TO

_____

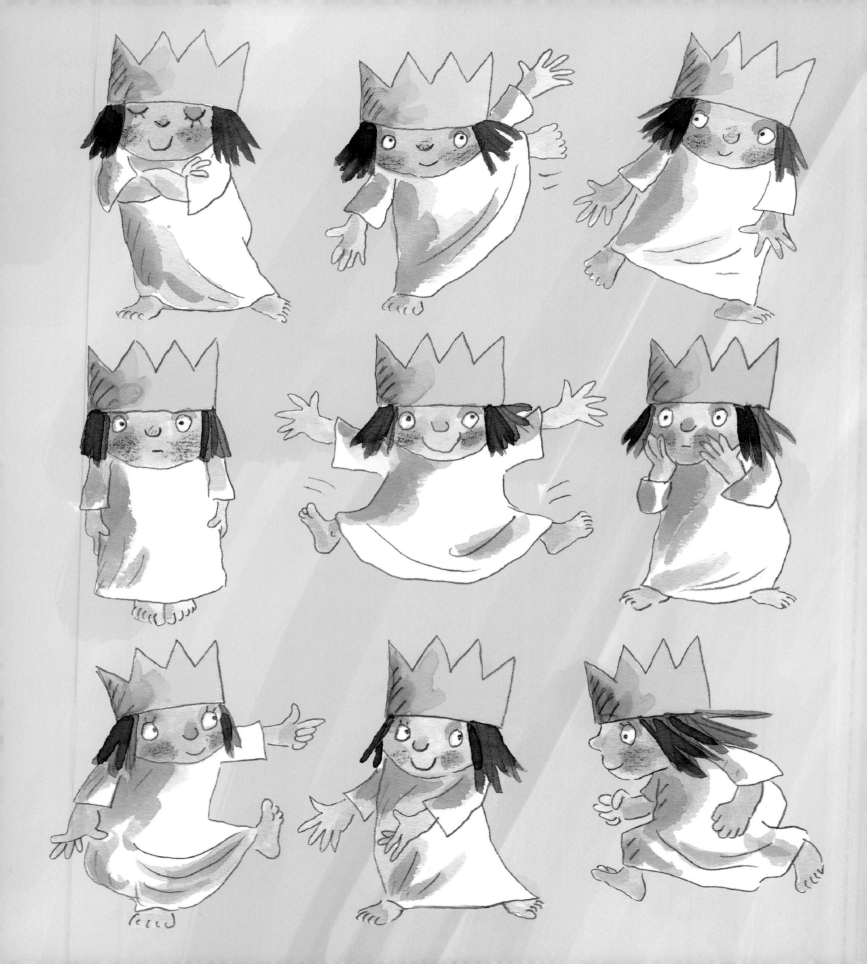

This paperback edition published in 2018 by Andersen Press Ltd.

First published in Great Britain in 2002 by Andersen Press Ltd.,

20 Vauxhall Bridge Road, London SW1V 2SA.

Text and Illustration copyright © Tony Ross, 2002

The rights of Tony Ross to be identified as the author and illustrator of this work have

been asserted by him in accordance with the Copyright, Designs and Patents Act, 1988.

All rights reserved.

Colour separated in Switzerland by Photolitho AG, Zürich.

Printed and bound in China.

Tony Ross has used pen, ink and watercolour in this book.

1   3   5   7   9   10   8   6   4   2

British Library Cataloguing in Publication Data available.

ISBN 978 1 78344 6 01 8

Little Princess

I Want My Tooth!

Tony Ross

Andersen Press

The Little Princess had WONDERFUL teeth.

She counted them every morning.
Then she cleaned them...

... then she counted them again.
She had TWENTY.

Some of her friends had fewer than twenty teeth.
But THEY were not ROYAL.

Her little brother, who WAS royal,
had NO teeth at all.

"Haven't I got wonderful teeth?" said the Little Princess.
"In smart straight lines," said the General.
"Shipshape and Bristol fashion," said the Admiral.

"Haven't I got wonderful teeth?" said the Little Princess.
"ROYAL teeth!" said the King.

So every night, the Little Princess cleaned
the royal teeth again.

"Your wonderful teeth are because
you eat all the right things," said the Cook.

"You can count them if you like," said the Little Princess.
"One... two... three... four..."

"HEY," said the Cook. "This one WOBBLES!"

"AAAAAGH!" screamed the Little Princess.
"One WOBBLES!"

"AAAAAGH!" screamed the Maid.
"One WOBBLES!"

The wobbly tooth wobbled MORE each day.

But the wobbly tooth didn't hurt, and soon
the Little Princess enjoyed wobbling it.

And she wobbled it and wobbled it, until the terrible
day the wobbly tooth disappeared.

"I WANT MY TOOTH!"
cried the Little Princess.

"You can have mine," said the Dentist,
"until your new one comes along!"
"I want my tooth NOW!" said the Little Princess.

Everybody in the Palace searched for the missing tooth...

... but it was NOWHERE to be found.
"I WANT MY TOOTH!" cried the Little Princess.

"SHE WANTS HER TOOTH!" cried the Maid.

"It's all right," said the Little Princess.
"I've FOUND it...

... HE'S got it!"

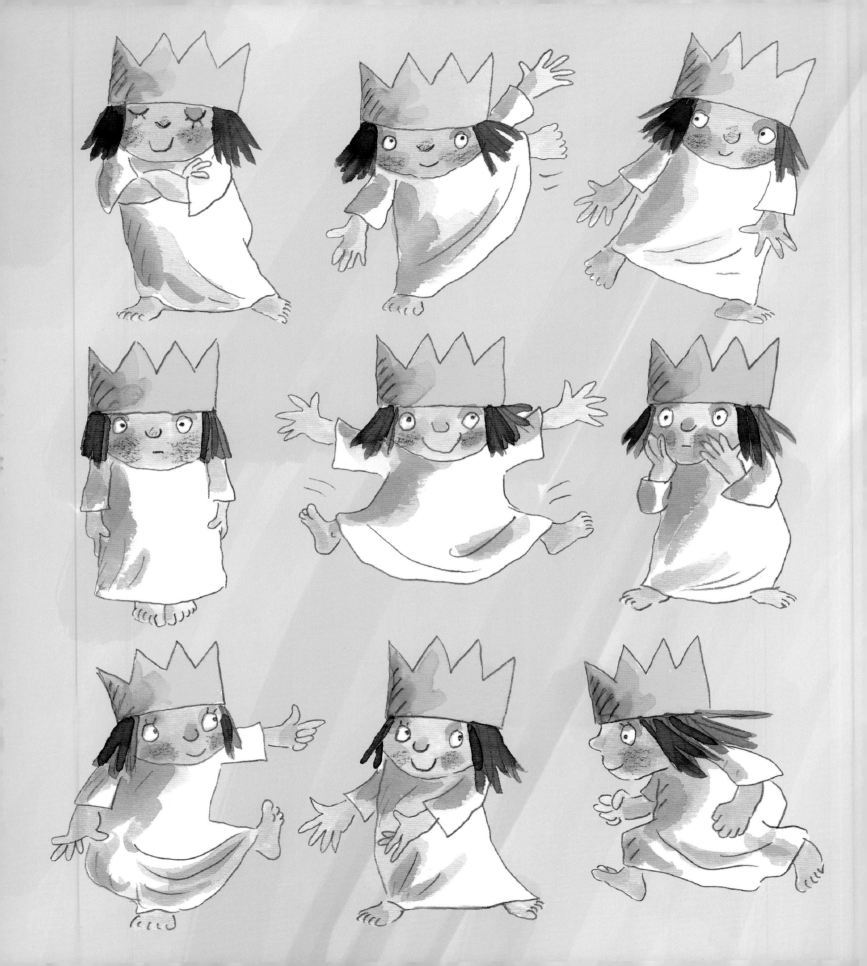

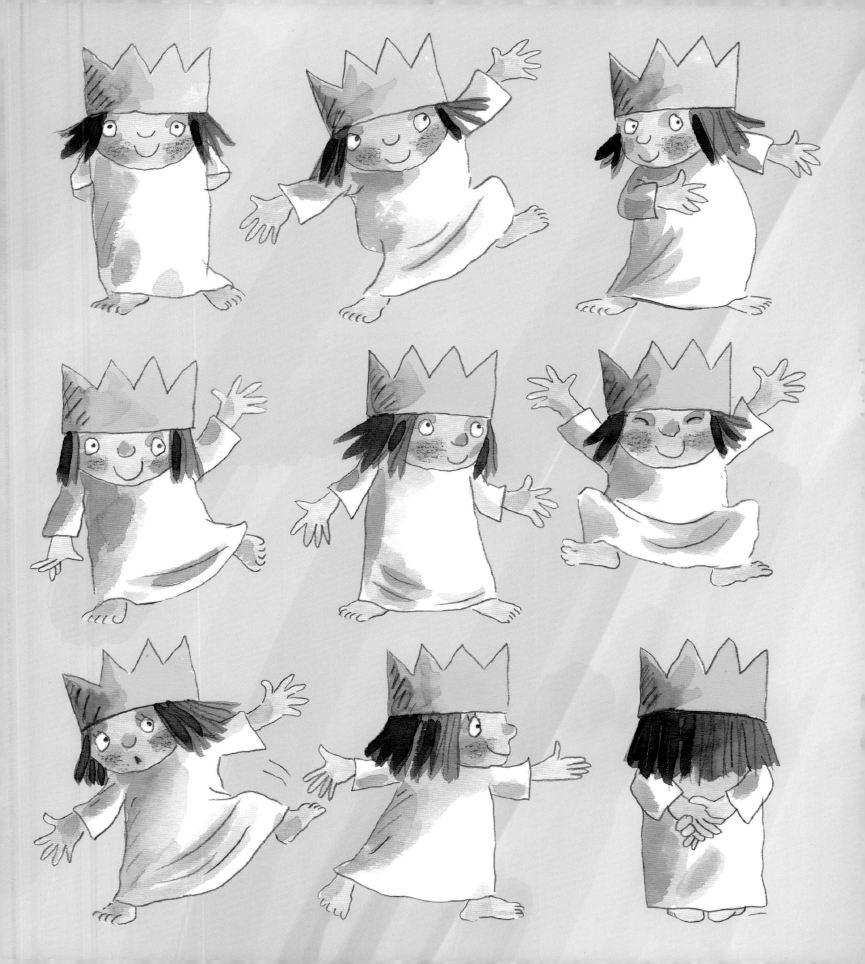